by Anna Kang   illustrated by Christopher Weyant

You Are (Not) Small

two lions

Published by Two Lions, New York.

www.apub.com

Amazon, the Amazon logo, and Two Lions are trademarks of Amazon.com, Inc., or its affiliates.

ISBN-13: 9781477847725 (hardcover)
ISBN-10: 1477847723 (hardcover)
ISBN-13: 9781477897720 (digital)
ISBN-10: 1477897720 (digital)

The illustrations are rendered in ink and watercolor with brush pens on Arches paper.

Book design by Katrina Damkoehler
Editor: Margery Cuyler

Printed in Mexico (R)
First edition
3 5 7 9 10 8 6 4 2

To Kate and Lily,
for inspiring us every day.
We love you exactly the way you are.

You are small.

I am not small.
You are big.

They are just like me.
You are small.

They are just like *me*.
You are big.

You are *all* small!

You are *all* big!

See? I am *not* small.

No, you are
not big.
You are big
and
you are small.

And you are
not small.
You are small
and
you are big.

I am hungry.

You are hairy.